# JAYDEN'S SECRET INGREDIENT

### Mélina Mangal

### Illustrated by **Ken Daley**

free spirit
PUBLISHING®

**Library of Congress Cataloging-in-Publication Data**
Names: Mangal, Mélina, author. | Daley, Ken, 1976- illustrator. | Mangal, Mélina. Jayden's impossible garden.
Title: Jayden's secret ingredient / Mélina Mangal ; illustrated by Ken Daley.
Description: Minneapolis, MN : Free Spirit Publishing, [2023] | Audience: Ages 4–10.
Identifiers: LCCN 2022052671 (print) | LCCN 2022052672 (ebook) | ISBN 9781631986024 (hardback) | ISBN 9781631986031 (ebook) |
    ISBN 9781631986048 (epub)
Subjects: CYAC: Gardening--Fiction. | Cooking--Fiction. | Scarlet runner bean--Fiction. | Beans--Fiction. | African Americans--Fiction. |
    Friendship--Fiction. | Neighbors--Fiction. | Courage--Fiction. | BISAC: JUVENILE FICTION / Social Themes / Friendship | JUVENILE FICTION /
    Diversity & Multicultural | LCGFT: Picture books.
Classification: LCC PZ7.1.M36466 Jd 2023  (print) | LCC PZ7.1.M36466 (ebook) | DDC [Fic]--dc23
LC record available at https://lccn.loc.gov/2022052671
LC ebook record available at https://lccn.loc.gov/2022052672

Edited by Alison Behnke
Cover and interior design by Courtenay Fletcher

Printed in China

**Free Spirit Publishing**
An imprint of Teacher Created Materials
9850 51st Avenue North, Suite 100
Minneapolis, MN 55442
(612) 338-2068
help4kids@freespirit.com
freespirit.com

For Mitali.
—MM

To my dad, Carl, a gardener at heart.
—Ken

Jayden watched a hummingbird sip nectar from the blossoms of the scarlet runner beans. He'd planted the vine with his neighbor Mr. Curtis, and it was growing strong.

"Morning, Jayden!" Mr. Curtis said as he entered the yard.
"Can you help me reach some beans?"

"Sure!" Jayden trotted over and started picking. "You want the flowers too?"

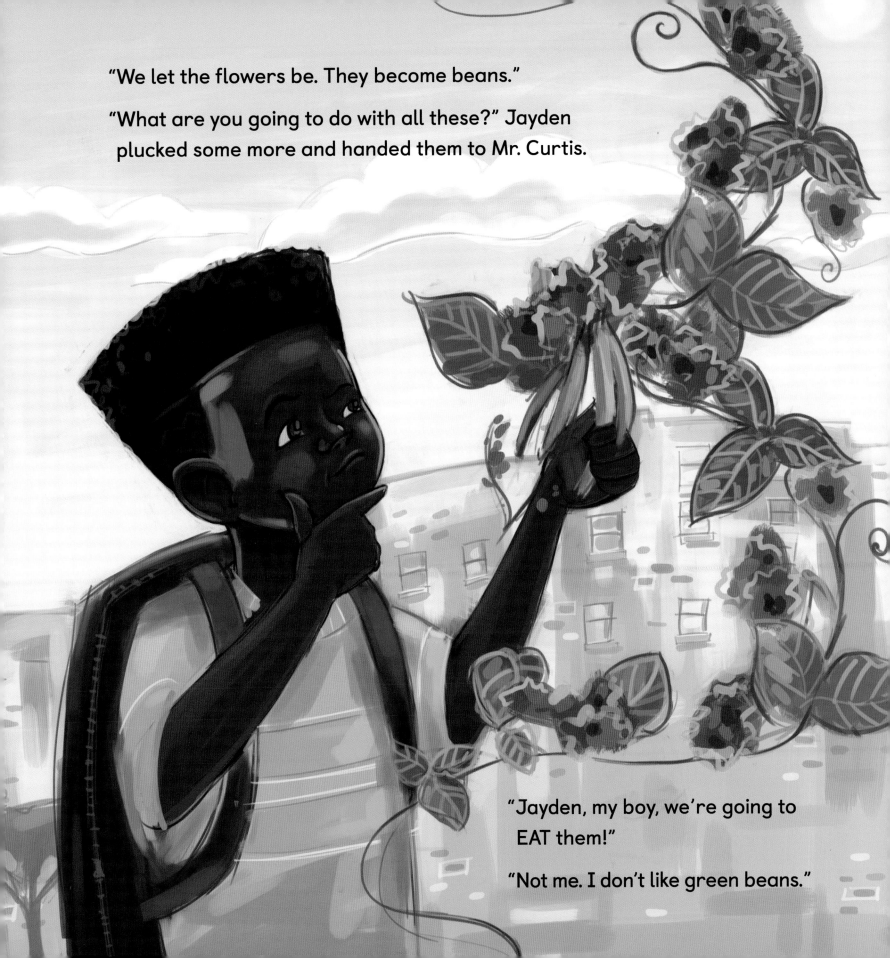

"We let the flowers be. They become beans."

"What are you going to do with all these?" Jayden plucked some more and handed them to Mr. Curtis.

"Jayden, my boy, we're going to EAT them!"

"Not me. I don't like green beans."

Mr. Curtis shook his head. "You've never had *these*. Tell you what—come over Sunday and I'll show you how to cook the best beans in the world."

All that day, Jayden thought about Mr. Curtis's invitation. He liked carrots and peas, and Mama's coleslaw and collard greens. But how could he get out of eating scarlet runner beans?

Saturday morning, Jayden saw Mr. Curtis near the fence again.

"I'll help," Jayden called.

Sheniece from down the hall approached with a bowl. "May I pick some beans from your vine?"

"Help yourself," Mr. Curtis said. "Just save us a taste. I love to try different dishes."

An idea popped into Jayden's head. *If everyone else eats the green beans, then I won't have to.* "Take as many as you want, Sheniece!"

Mr. Curtis smiled. "That's mighty kind of you, Jayden."

Jayden felt bad. Mr. Curtis didn't know what he was *really* thinking.

"Don't forget to come over with your Mama tomorrow, son.
You'll taste something special."

Jayden didn't want to disappoint Mr. Curtis.
But how could green beans taste special?

Jayden almost forgot about the beans as he did his homework. He read about an adventurous scientist who traveled the world, learning about new plants.

Jayden looked out his window. Bunches of beans hung from the scarlet runner vines.

*That's it!*

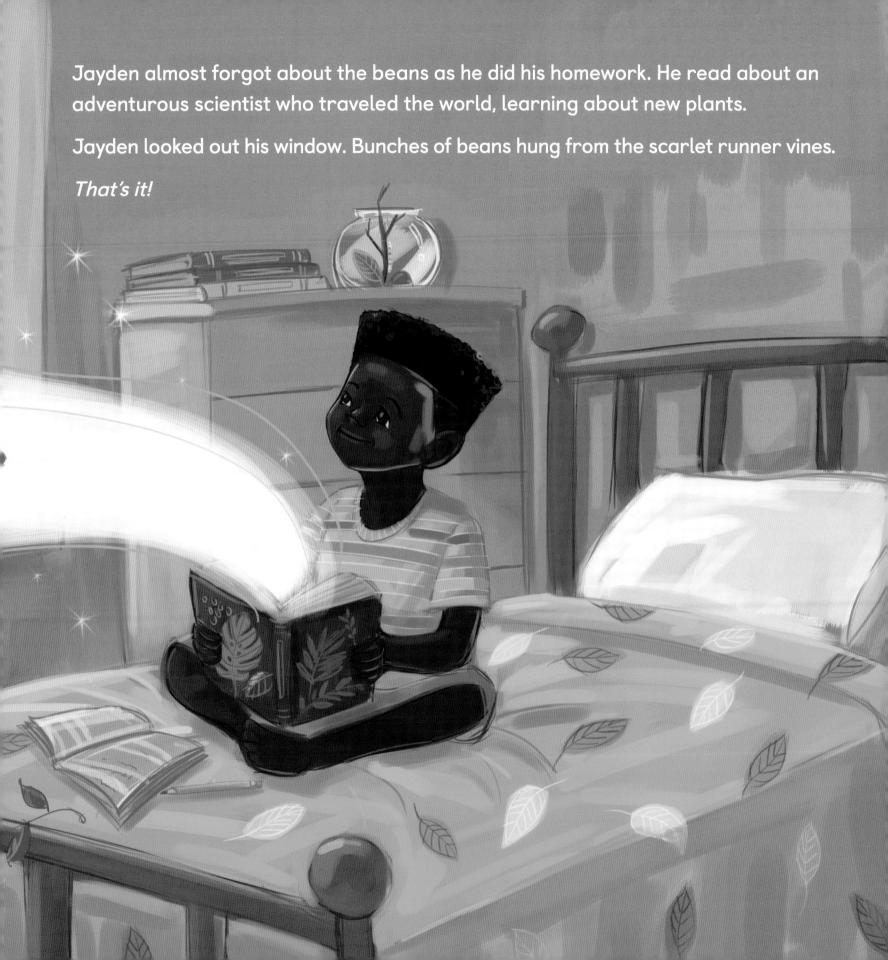

He ran outside and harvested every bean he could see.

"Free green beans!" Jayden called to Mr. Vu and his children.

"We'd love to try them," Mr. Vu said.

"Take all of them!" Jayden said.

"This is enough for us. Kids, say thank you to Jayden."

Then Mrs. Fournier came around the corner from her walk.

"Free beans!" Jayden offered.

"Hi, Jayden. Did you grow these?" she asked.

"Yes," Jayden answered. "With Mr. Curtis."

"I love green beans," Mrs. Fournier said.
"Thank you."

Jayden still had half a bowl left.

Just then, a familiar silver car pulled up. It was Mr. Curtis's daughter.

"Free green beans!" Jayden shouted.

"I'll take them," she said. "Thank you."

Jayden smiled. *No more beans!*

The next evening, Mama called out, "Ready for dinner with Mr. Curtis? Smells like my crockpot chicken is done."

"Mama, I don't like green beans," Jayden said. "But I don't want Mr. Curtis to feel bad."

"Have you ever tried scarlet runner beans?" Mama asked.

Jayden shook his head.

"Well, neither have I. This will be an adventure for both of us!"

"Just in time!" Mr. Curtis said as he opened the door. "Jayden, you can help me cook. Oh, and my daughter brought me the beans you picked. Thank you."

Mr. Curtis showed Jayden how to snap, clean, and steam the beans. He drizzled a little olive oil and gave Jayden a spoon. Jayden felt like a real chef.

"When I was your age, I didn't like green beans," Mr. Curtis said. "Didn't like all the other stuff folks cooked with them."

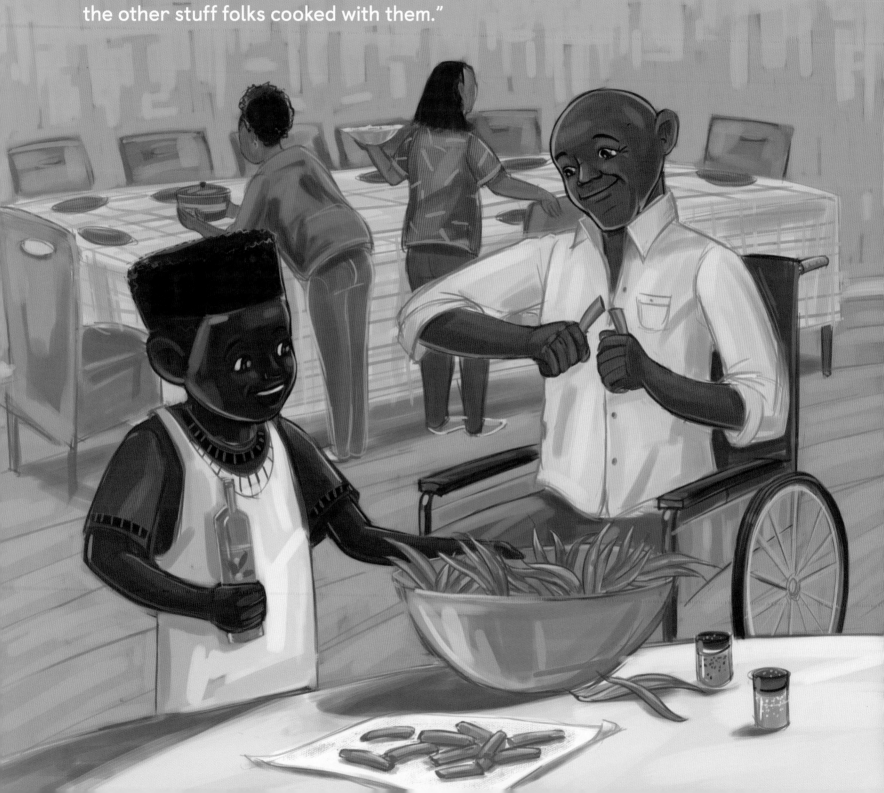

Jayden looked at Mr. Curtis with surprise.

As Mr. Curtis spooned the beans into a bowl, someone knocked on the door.

Soon, neighbors had gathered around the table, each with a different dish.

Jayden felt a little queasy. *So many green beans!*

"Thank you for sharing," said Sheniece. "My mom and I cooked the scarlet runners with smoked turkey and vinegar."

Mr. Vu said, "I made my beans with garlic, sesame, and pepper flakes."

"I used garlic too, and also butter and parsley," said Mrs. Fournier.

Mr. Curtis looked at Jayden. "Tell them what's in ours."

Jayden felt proud hearing the word *ours*. "Just beans, olive oil, and salt and pepper."

Mr. Curtis smiled. "And one secret ingredient. You'll know it after you try them."

Jayden watched as his neighbors and Mama all spooned food onto their plates. Everyone took a little bit of everything.

*I'll be adventurous, like the scientist I read about*, thought Jayden. *I'll try something new.*

Mama nodded at Jayden as he took a deep breath and began tasting.

"Jayden, my boy, what's your favorite?"

Jayden didn't think any of them were bad. He even *liked* some of the beans! But he pointed to the dish they'd made together.

"I told you. Nothing like beans fresh from the vine."

"But what's the secret ingredient?"

"Courage," Mr. Curtis said, "to try something new!"

Jayden looked at the vines outside the window, the green bean pods dripping down, and the faces of his neighbors all around.

"You forgot one more ingredient, Mr. Curtis."

"What's that?"

Jayden beamed. "Friendship!"

# A NOTE FROM THE AUTHOR

When I was a kid, I didn't particularly care for green beans. They were a disappointing dull green, unlike the bright picture on the can, and they were mushy. I still ate them, and I enjoyed them more than some other vegetables, but it wasn't until I was away at college that I first tasted fresh green beans. That was an experience I'll never forget. A whole new world had opened up to me—the world of fresh produce.

Like many kids, I was raised eating canned fruits and vegetables. They're often cheaper than fresh, and they keep for a long time on the shelf, which is especially convenient when you have a big family. In the Midwest where I grew up, fresh vegetables just weren't plentiful at the grocery stores in the winter months. And they were more expensive.

As Jayden learns, it takes time and work to grow vegetables you can eat. But the taste alone is worth it. Fresh vegetables are more flavorful and more nutritious. You can grow your own, starting out with just a few potted plants, as Jayden and Mr. Curtis do. Gardening is a fun activity, no matter what you grow.

There are also many other options for eating more fresh veggies, like going to a local farmer's market, joining a food co-op or community-supported agriculture (CSA) program, or simply browsing through the fresh produce section at the grocery store. And if your school offers fresh fruits or veggies, try them. You might be surprised at what you like!

Wherever you get your vegetables, try preparing them in different ways. It's fun to discover what flavors you like best.

## Beautiful Beans

Scarlet runner beans are beautiful. In fact, so are bean plants in general. Bean plants produce flowers, which then become the bean pods you can eat as green beans. And most beans can be eaten dried too. If you leave the bean pods or green beans on the plant until they dry, you can collect the dried beans inside and eat them cooked. They keep longer this way, so you can grow beans in the summer and eat them all year round.

Beans are packed with protein, and you can eat cooked dried beans instead of meat as a source of this important nutrient. You need protein to build your muscles and stay strong. Beans also have other essential nutrients like iron, potassium, and zinc.

So whether you're eating beans fresh or dried, you can appreciate the many ways to enjoy them and the many ways they help your body!

# Recipes

In this story, Jayden discovers lots of ways to eat beans. He also finds out that everyone has different tastes. You can learn more about your own preferences by trying some of the recipes from Jayden's neighbors. Though Jayden and his neighbors used scarlet runner beans, you can use any type of green bean for these recipes. One thing to know is that cooking times for beans will vary depending on the type of beans, whether they're freshly picked, and even the pan you use. And of course, any beans can be cooked longer to match your preferences and taste. Have a grown-up help you, and enjoy preparing fresh beans together!

## MR. CURTIS'S BEANS

### Ingredients

- 2 cups green beans, or 30–40 fresh-picked bean pods
- 1 tablespoon olive oil
- Salt and black pepper to taste

### Directions

1. Snap off the stem ends of the green beans and throw the ends away or compost them.
2. Put the bean pods in a colander and rinse them thoroughly in a clean kitchen sink.
3. Gently pat the beans dry with a clean kitchen towel.
4. Put the olive oil in a shallow skillet or frying pan on the stovetop.
5. Turn on the burner to medium-high.

6. Add the green beans to the pan and lightly toss with a large spoon, making sure the beans are coated in the oil.
7. Sauté the beans for about 5 minutes.
8. Turn off the stove and cover the pan with a lid.
9. Keep the pan covered on the stove and let the beans cook for about 10 minutes more, until they are tender but still bright green.
10. Add a little salt and black pepper to taste, and serve.

***Serves 4***

## MR. VU'S BEANS

### Ingredients

- 2 cups green beans, or 30–40 fresh-picked bean pods
- 1 tablespoon olive oil
- 1 tablespoon finely chopped garlic
- 1 tablespoon soy sauce
- 1 tablespoon rice vinegar
- 1 tablespoon honey
- 1 teaspoon sesame oil
- Chili flakes, to taste (optional)

### Directions

1. Snap off the stem ends of the green beans and throw the ends away or compost them.

2. Put the bean pods in a colander and rinse them thoroughly in a clean kitchen sink.

3. Gently pat the beans dry with a clean kitchen towel.

4. Fill a large pot with 12 to 16 cups of water. Place it on the stovetop.

5. Turn the burner on high and cover the pot to bring the water to a boil.

6. Remove the lid, and carefully add the cleaned green beans to the boiling water. Blanch the beans in the boiling water for 3 to 4 minutes. (*Blanch* means to cook something in very hot water for a short time, or to parboil it.)

7. Turn off the burner. Carefully remove the beans from the boiling water using a slotted spoon. Put them into a colander and rinse the beans under cold running water to prevent overcooking. Then drain them and set them aside.

8. Add the olive oil to a wok or other large pan on the stovetop.

9. Turn on the burner to medium-high, and add the chopped garlic.

10. Sauté the garlic for about 1 minute.

11. Turn off the burner. Add the soy sauce, rice vinegar, honey, sesame oil, and chili flakes (if you're using them). Toss gently.

12. Add the blanched green beans to the pan and stir until well coated with the seasonings, then serve.

*Serves 4*

# SHENIECE'S DOWN-HOME BEANS

## Ingredients

- 2 cups green beans, or 30–40 fresh-picked bean pods
- 1 smoked turkey bone
- 3 tablespoons apple cider vinegar
- 1 tablespoon sugar
- 1 teaspoon salt

## Directions

1. Snap off the stem ends of the green beans and throw the ends away or compost them.

2. Put the bean pods in a colander and rinse them thoroughly in a clean kitchen sink.

3. Gently pat the beans dry with a clean kitchen towel.

4. Fill a large pot with 12 to 16 cups of water.

5. Place the smoked turkey bone into the pot, along with the apple cider vinegar, sugar, and salt.

6. Turn the heat on high and bring everything to a boil. Once the mixture is boiling, turn the heat down to low and cook for 45 minutes.

7. When the meat is falling off the turkey bone, add the green beans to the water and simmer for 20 minutes. They will get quite soft.

8. Carefully remove the green beans with a slotted spoon. Serve them with or without the turkey bits, according to your preference.

*Serves 4*

## MRS. FOURNIER'S GREEN BEANS

*Ingredients*

- 2 cups green beans, or 30–40 fresh-picked bean pods
- 1 tablespoon butter
- 1 tablespoon finely chopped garlic
- 1 teaspoon chopped parsley
- Salt and black pepper to taste

*Directions*

1. Snap off the stem ends of the green beans and throw the ends away or compost them.
2. Put the bean pods in a colander and rinse them thoroughly in a clean kitchen sink.
3. Gently pat the beans dry with a clean kitchen towel.
4. Place beans in a medium pan or skillet. Fill the pan with just enough water to cover the green beans, and place it on the stovetop.
5. Bring to a boil over high heat. Then reduce the heat to low and simmer for about 10 minutes or until all the water has cooked off.
6. Turn off the stove and add butter and chopped garlic to the pan. Toss gently.
7. Turn stove back on very low and sauté for a couple of minutes.
8. Cover and let cook for 5 more minutes.
9. Stir in parsley, along with salt and black pepper to taste, and serve.

*Serves 4*

## How do *you* like to eat green beans?

If you have a favorite recipe, you can share it with me at my website, melinamangal.com.

# ABOUT THE AUTHOR AND ILLUSTRATOR

Writing at the intersection of nature, literature, and culture, **Mélina Mangal** highlights young people whose voices are rarely heard and the people and places that inspire them to explore their world. She is the author of short stories and biographies for young people, including *The Vast Wonder of the World: Biologist Ernest Everett Just,* winner of the Carter G. Woodson Book Award and named an NCSS/CBC Notable Social Studies Trade Book for Young People. This is her second book about Jayden—the first, *Jayden's Impossible Garden*, was also illustrated by Ken Daley. Mélina also works as a school library teacher in Minnesota and enjoys spending time outdoors with her family, whether it's in her backyard or hiking in the woods. Visit her online at melinamangal.com.

**Ken Daley** is an artist and an award-winning illustrator of the picture books *Jayden's Impossible Garden, Joseph's Big Ride,* and *Auntie Luce's Talking Paintings* (Kirkus Review and Américas Award Honorable Mention). Ken draws inspiration for his work from his African-Caribbean roots, his life experiences, and the people and cultures he encounters along the way. Ken was born in Cambridge, Ontario, Canada, and currently lives with his wife and two pets in Rhode Island. You can visit him at kendaleyart.com.